Torben Kuhlmann was born in Germany in 1982.
He studied illustration and design at the University for Applied
Sciences in Hamburg with a focus on book illustration. His first work,
Lindbergh – The Tale of a Flying Mouse, quickly became a best seller and owes
its inventiveness to Torben's great enthusiasm for unusual mechanical
inventions. *Moletown* is his second book for NorthSouth.

Copyright © 2015 by NordSüd Verlag AG, CH-8005 Zürich, Switzerland.
English translation copyright © 2015 by NorthSouth Books Inc., New York 10016.
Illustrations, text, and book design by Torben Kuhlmann.
Translated by Andrew Rushton.

First published in the United States, Great Britain, Canada, Australia, and New Zealand in 2015
by NorthSouth Books, Inc., an imprint of NordSüd Verlag AG, CH-8005 Zürich, Switzerland.

Distributed in the United States by NorthSouth Books Inc., New York 10016.
Library of Congress Cataloging-in-Publication Data is available.
ISBN: 978-0-7358-4208-3 (trade edition)
Printed in Germany by Grafisches Centrum Cuno GmbH & Co. KG, Calbe, December 2015.
3 5 7 9 • 10 8 6 4 2
www.northsouth.com

FSC
www.fsc.org
MIX
Paper from
responsible sources
FSC® C043106

Torben Kuhlmann

MOLETOWN

North
South

The story of Moletown began many years ago.
One day a mole moved under a lush green meadow.
He was alone at first, but not for long. And over
time, life underground changed. . . .

Do Not Disturb

Many generations later, the moles' green
meadow had completely disappeared. Almost.